The Laziest CROCODILE in AUSTRALIA

Written and illustrated by

Michael Salmon

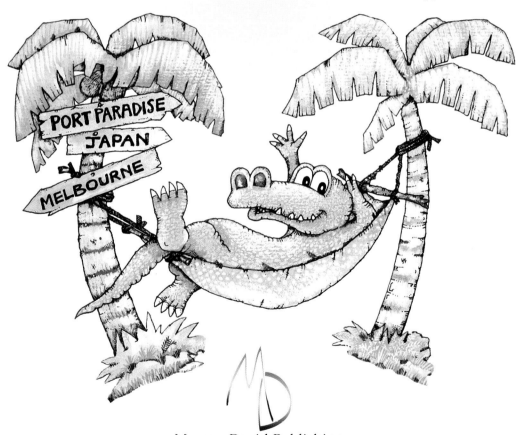

PORT PARADISE

JAPAN

MELBOURNE

Murray David Publishing

35 Borgnis Street, Davidson, New South Wales, 2085, Australia, P.O. Box 140, Belrose West, New South Wales, 2085, Australia
Phone: 61 2 9451 3895   Fax: 61 2 9452 3663   Email: mail@m2d.com.au   www.m2d.com.au
Publishing Director: Marion Child, Marketing Director: David Jenkins, Executive Director: David Forsythe, Production Manager: Simone Coupland
Copyright © Monster Promotions Pty Ltd, 2009, Copyright © in Layout M2D Publishing Pty Ltd, 2009
This large format edition first published 2009
Designed by Simone Coupland
ISBN: 978-1-877009-23-5   Printed in Indonesia

Near the very top of Australia, in the far north of Queensland, lies the town of Port Paradise, known by the locals as 'Port'. It's hard to find on a map because its name is always printed in tiny letters. Mangroves cluster in the swamp along the Paradise River, and on the other side of town sandy coral beaches stretch to the horizon.

The steep hills behind Port are covered with ancient tropical rainforest. Bright butterflies flit amongst the strange and beautiful plants or settle on exotic flowers. The shady heart of the forest is alive with animals and birds, sheltering from the hot northern sun.

Port is a quiet, relaxed sort of town. Nobody hurries, or seems to do very much except sit in the shade of the palm trees and gossip, or sip fresh pineapple juice or coconut milk. The shopkeepers only open their shops for a few hours, unless a tourist bus arrives of course.

Sometimes pale-faced strangers, lost in their rent-a-cars from down south, stumble across Port. The locals are happy to show them the souvenir shop, then after they've bought lots of painted shells and coral necklaces, the helpful townsfolk show them the way out of town.

Salt-water crocodiles have always lived in the swamp across the Paradise River. They like to doze on the warm river bank or play games amongst the mangrove trees. When it gets too hot, they slide into the cool slimy mud and tell crocodile jokes while they munch on mud crabs.

The crocodiles never had much to do with the people from Port, except when the Spot-A-Croc tourist boat chugged past each week. Then the crocodiles put on a special show, thrashing their tails, snapping their ferocious jaws, and doing the famous crocodile roll. The tourists loved it, and did a lot of snapping themselves, but only with their cameras. Next day the tour operator would reward the crocodiles with a big basket of fried chicken.

It was a job all the crocodiles enjoyed…all except one.
Les was the laziest crocodile that had ever lived. His favourite
pastime was to do absolutely nothing! He'd made himself
a hammock from the vines and grasses, and tied it to some
trees a long way from the other crocodiles so their chatter
and splashing wouldn't disturb his sleep. After each nap
he would lazily open one eye and gaze across the river, idly
sharpening his teeth with an old file he'd got from a cane-
cutter years ago. He was proud of his razor-sharp teeth, and
even today he could bite through almost anything…if he
wanted to, that is.

The other crocodiles made up Lazy Les jokes while he slept, and laughed till they cried, but they were careful not to tell them too loudly…not with those teeth of his.

None of the crocodiles new that life was going to change for all of them, including Les.

Early one morning a sleek cabin cruiser slid quietly past Port Paradise and stopped near the mangrove swamp. The rattle of chains woke the crocodiles as the anchors dropped into the water. They had never seen such a big boat, and swam around admiring it from all angles. Even Les opened an eye and glanced at the gleaming paint-work. 'More tourists,' he muttered to himself, and rolled over in his hammock and slept.

Out onto the deck stepped Mr Yen, the famous Japanese hotel builder and real estate tycoon. He was followed by his huge sumo bodyguards, Fuji and Yama.

'This is the perfect place for a new Yen Luxury hotel,' he cried, pointing excitedly at the swamp. 'Hey, you crocodiles,' he shouted through his megaphone, 'you're very lucky. I'll give you lots and lots of lovely fish every day if you let me build my hotel here.'

The crocodiles all nodded their snouts eagerly. It sounded almost too good to be true.

But there was a problem. As soon as the people of Port Paradise heard about Mr Yen's plans they became annoyed for all sorts of reasons. Some didn't want a big hotel nearby. Others wanted to know who owned the swamp anyway, and who was going to be paid for the use of it.

'Those stupid crocodiles have lived in that swamp for thousands of years,' said the pie shop owner, 'but they still don't know a thing about business.'

'Fancy giving it all away for a pile of fish,' grumbled the lady from the T-shirt boutique. 'They could have made a fortune,' she added, 'and passed some onto us!'

Mr Yen was a very clever business man. He invited the shopkeepers for a cocktail party on board his boat and asked some of the crocodiles to help serve the drinks and savoury seaweed snacks.

When everyone had had plenty to drink and people were beginning to feel happy and sleepy, Fuji and Yama unrolled a large plan of the hotel. It had everything—a golf course, swimming pool, tennis courts, marina, and a little scenic railway to take visitors up into the rainforest. Everyone was very impressed.

'The Swamp Regency will be the best hotel in Australia,' beamed Mr Yen. 'Tourists have lots of money, so you will soon be very rich! Port Paradise will be world famous.'

When the other crocodiles moved up river to their new home, Les refused to go. 'No way I'm moving, sport,' he said. 'I didn't agree to your stupid deal, so push off and leave me in peace,' and he rolled over and was soon snoring happily.

'He must be the laziest crocodile in the world,' said one crocodile to another. 'And the silliest,' she replied, munching happily on one of Mr Yen's fresh fish.

'**VROOM! CRASH! THUD!**' A huge yellow bulldozer roared through the mangroves, flattening everything before it.

'Oi, mate!' yelled Les, 'give a bloke a chance to get a bit of shut-eye! You can't...' Too late. The dozers big blade crushed one of the trees supporting Les' hammock, and down he tumbled. Furious, he snapped at one of the big wheels as it thundered past, slicing through the rubber tyre with his razor sharp teeth.

'**BANG!**' The enormous machine shuddered to a halt, but before the driver knew what had happened, Les was nowhere to be seen.

Les was upset. His riverbank home was gone, his hammock was ruined—where could he go for his next croc-nap? He floated over to Mr Yen's boat and he crept up and over the side.

'Nobody about,' murmured Les, as he slithered into Mr Yen's cabin and climbed onto his bed.

'Mmm, not bad at all,' said Les, helping himself to Mr Yen's sushi and sashimi. 'This bloke really knows how to live,' and he settled down to sleep.

'What! What's going on?' yelled Mr Yen. 'You bad crocodile —how dare you sleep in my cabin! Fuji! Yama! Throw him out!'

'Oi!' Les grumbled as the big sumo wrestlers dragged him to the side of the boat, 'I didn't agree to your deal! I'm not going any-w-h-e-e-e-r-e…' **SPLASH!**

Les hardly slept over the next few days—the noisy builders worked around the clock on the new hotel. He mooched off away from the racket and came upon a smooth grassy hillock. 'At last,' he sighed, settling down for a sleep beside a tiny flagpole sticking out of a hole in the ground.

'**THWACK!**' A golfball hit him hard on the snout.

'Yeeow!' yelled Les, still half asleep, as Mr Yen came running up waving a golf club.

'You lazy bones! You good for nothing crocodile!' Mr Yen fumed, whacking Les with his golfclub. 'You ruined my hole in one!'

Fuji and Yama 'escorted' Les off the course.

'Come back again,' growled Fuji, 'and we'll turn you into a handbag and shoes!'

'They can't do this to me,' fumed Les, glaring at the half-built hotel. 'I'm a protected species!'

Mr Yen and his bodyguards were lazing about in the new pool beside the hotel. Les inspected the metal grill that separated the pool from the ocean.

'I'll give them a bit of a hurry-up,' muttered Les as he bit through the padlock and lifted the grill out of the water and hid amongst some plastic plants. He didn't have to wait long.

'**SWOOSH!**' Shark fins broke the surface, heading straight for Mr Yen, Fuji and Yama.

'Yeeoow!' Big fish in the water! Quick!' The three broke all Olympic records as they rushed across the pool.

Dark clouds approached, and Les hurried into a funny little cabin to shelter from the passing tropical shower. Soon he was snoring his snout off.

'**TOOT TOOT!**' Les was jolted awake. The cabin was moving!

It was a carriage in Mr Yen's Puff Puff train—his favourite toy. Les peered out the side. A long strip of rainforest had been scraped off the mountainside so that tourists could visit the 'jungle' in comfort.

'I'm off,' said Les, and clambered out of the carriage. He looked up to the top of the mountain where the train was slowly puffing along, then down to the other end of the track where it ended at a little station by the river. Les had an idea.

Gripping the railway line in his strong jaws he wrenched the rails away from the sleeper, bending them to one side till the ends stuck out over the edge of the river bank.

'Hope they've got good brakes,' smirked Les,' or they'll be in the drink.'

Les was exhausted. He'd never had so much exercise in his life before. 'Where can I have a little siesta?' he murmured. The beach on the far side of Port Paradise was too hot, and the only fish that swam there were tasteless jellyfish. He swam idly back towards his favourite old haunt—the cool, muddy swamp.

The hotel was finished. It loomed over the swamp water supported by countless sturdy wooden pylons. In the setting sun it looked very grand and very new with its big neon sign flashing and its plastic palm trees waving.

Les could see Mr Yen welcoming his jet-setter guests as they arrived from all over the world for the grand opening. He dived deep and finally surfaced under the marina. Delicious smells wafted from the kitchens.

'Mmmm, smells good,' murmured Les. 'I could go a few prawns right now, but how can I get to them?'

The party had begun. All the Port shopkeepers were there in their best clothes, and the guests were dressed in national costume. It was the Arabs in the disco who gave Les the idea. He 'borrowed' a small sail from one of the yachts. 'Look out tucker, here I come!'

Les marched up to Mr Yen. 'G'day—how're yer doin' mate, I'm Les from Melbourne' (it was the only foreign sounding place he knew). His disguise was working. Les headed for the food.

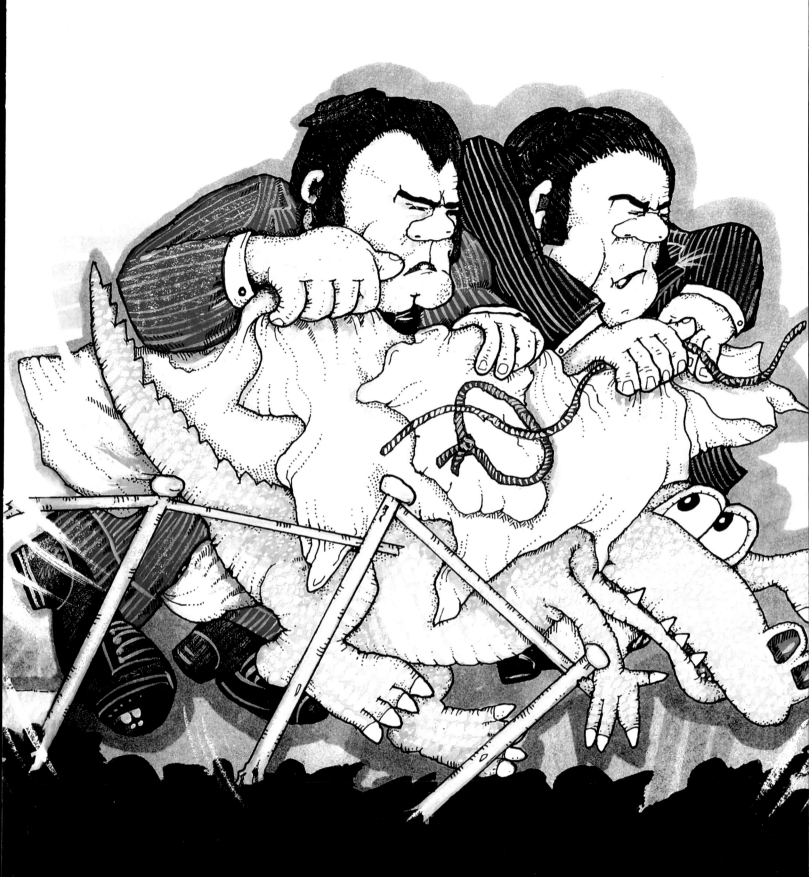

'Got you, you pesky crocodile!' Fuji and Yama had spotted Les' tail trailing behind him. 'Now it's handbag and matching belt time for you…and perhaps a pair of crocodile-skin shoes!'

Les twisted out of their hands, crashed through the hand rail and dived into the sea.

Les held his breath for as long as he could then finally surfaced amongst the pylons supporting the hotel. Everyone was enjoying themselves, eating, drinking…making too much noise for Les to go to sleep, and besides, he was hungry. He snapped at one of the pylons, and before long he had gnawed his way through. He tried another, and another…

CREEAK...CRACK! With a loud splintering noise the hotel slowly tilted forward into the water. The lights went out, people screamed and dashed about, but the band kept playing as if nothing had happened. It was only when one of the guests stepped out of the hotel and straight into the sea that Mr Yen realised what had happened. His beautiful hotel had collapsed and was floating like a raft.

When the guests stepped out onto the decks of their yachts next morning, the Swamp Regency was nowhere to be seen. Mr Yen was suspicious about the chewed pylons, but there wasn't any sign of a crocodile, only plastic grass and potplants and a few champagne corks bobbing about where his hotel had been.

'Take the helicopter,' he said to Fuji, 'and see if you can find the hotel.' The guests and the people of Port Paradise watched as Mr Yen and Yama set out for the open sea in search of a floating hotel.

But alas, the hotel was no longer floating. It had struck the Great Barrier Reef and sunk. The reef fish couldn't believe their luck—an underwater hotel just for them. Fuji circled the sunken hotel once then prepared to land on the boat's helipad.

Mr Yen shook his head sadly. 'Never again will I try to build anything in Australia,' he said and headed for New Zealand to see if there was any land there that he could buy from the sheep.

Life soon returned to normal in Port Paradise, though some of the shopkeepers looked wistfully out to sea now and then. The hotel site became a muddy mangrove swamp again, rainforest grew back over the railway track, and the crocodiles returned from up-river.

As for Les, well, he made himself another hammock further up the river bank and became lazier than ever. Too lazy to ever tell the other crocodiles what had happened to their daily fish supply!